To Shirley

"God Bless you!"

RayE murray

MOSES' ROD

RAY E. MURRAY

authorHOUSE®

AuthorHouse™
1663 Liberty Drive
Bloomington, IN 47403
www.authorhouse.com
Phone: 1-800-839-8640

First published by AuthorHouse   3/17/2010

ISBN: 978-1-4490-8957-3 (e)
ISBN: 978-1-4490-8955-9 (sc)
ISBN: 978-1-4490-8956-6 (hc)

Library of Congress Control Number: 2010903444

Printed in the United States of America
Bloomington, Indiana

This book is printed on acid-free paper.

Scripture if from King James Version

DEDICATION

To my loving wife, Carol
and our four children Terry, Timmy, Rusty and Shirley
and their children and all the future generations that
come from this family tree, this book is for you
Thanks to my pastor, Dan Hollifield and his wife, Patricia for
their encouragement to me to have this work published.
Some of the ideas here came from Dan's preaching
(And he thought no one was listening)

"Quiet often it is not the lofty ideals of theology that causes us to pause and ponder the truth of God's word, but the everyday happenings that surround us. Within the pages of this book those very happenings are found in abundance."
Dan Hollifield, Pastor Pilgrim Baptist Church

CHAPTER 1

SOMEONE WAS INSIDE HIS HEAD. They had a big hammer. They were beating and causing considerable pain. Gotta make them stop. He managed to pry open one eye and discovered that the light in the room was blinding which caused the pain to increase. With a groan he managed to pry himself up.

"Finally decided to join the living, did you?" He didn't recognize the voice and although it hadn't been that loud, it added to his misery,

"What – what happened? Where am I? What am I doing here?" Whatever was going on, he had not a clue.

"Well sir, last night you came in, waving around this big jug of the meanest white lightning that's available. Pure corn. You kept hitting that jug and saying, "My name is Jonah and this is my whale!" You took on too much and passed out. I carried you in here and put you to bed. Had to mop the floor where you upchucked."

That had been last fall. It was his first encounter with corn whiskey and he had sworn that it would also be his last. He knew. There was no point in running. There was no where to go. God had selected him. He had been called into God's ministry.

Gathering up his courage, he had sought out the minister just off campus. There he poured out his heart and confessed what he had done. "Oh, such a wonderful, scary thing it is. Many of us have had to stop running." His smile was sincere and that helped ease the pain.

Then, there was the going home from school and sharing the news with his parents. "Son, are you sure? Are you very, very sure? This is something not to be entered into lightly." Dad was like that. Be sure you know what you're doing before you jump in.

Mom simply grabbed him in a big hug. With tears running down her cheeks, she said, "I'm so proud of you son. You'll make a fine minister."

Dad had made contact with a minister friend of his. Taking me in hand, he had made the journey with me to the city. He wanted me to stay with Rev. Birchfield and be his assistant for a while before I ventured out on my own.

This did not set well with me. I wanted to go forth now. No waiting around. Turn me loose and let me go. After all, what could this old man possibly teach me? I was sure that God would give me everything I would ever need.

I guess Rev. Birchfield was a lot smarter than I had given him credit for. He surely knew what I was thinking as he began to question me. "There's a lot more to being a pastor of a church than just preaching son. That's number one. All these other things that are so important. Do you know how to conduct a wedding? Can you easily find the right words of comfort for a family who just lost a loved one? How do you council that young couple that is about to wed or what do you say to them if they are about to separate? And, you must always remember, never put yourself in a position where you are alone with a member of the opposite sex."

My mind began to reel as he brought up all these things. All I wanted to do was go out somewhere and preach. Now, I quickly realized that it wasn't going to work that way for me.

Several weeks later, Rev. Birchfield announced to his church that I would be bringing the message the next Sunday. I was excited. I was worried. I prayed to God to guide me and help me. He heard me. I found the scripture. I prepared the message. A good, short message that shouldn't last over thirty five or forty minutes.

That's one thing Rev. Birchfield had been trying to teach me. Have an exciting opening to your message. Have a spirit filled ending to the message. Keep the two parts as close together as possible.

Sunday morning came. I was ready! I was ready, wasn't I ? The choir finished the last song and Rev. Birchfield announced that Rev. Joseph Edgar Hendrix would be bringing the message this morning and that it was his first time to preach.

Nothing to be nervous about, I tried to tell my shaking knees as I made my way to the podium. I looked up and there they were. Dad and mom and my sister. Right there. On the front pew. Thank you God. I had made notes and now my mind was as blank as a clean sheet of paper.

With my bible and notes in hand, I gathered myself and began. I read the scripture. I began my sermon. I preached the entire message. I found the closing notes that I had so carefully prepared. I closed out my message and gave the invitation. As the choir sang the hymn, I checked the time. My thirty five minute message, counting the time the choir sang, had lasted ten minutes.

Rev. Birchfield had told my family. They were there to support me and wish me well. After a nice visit and a delicious meal prepared by Mrs. Birchfield, my dad brought out a package for me. "I know how much you enjoy hunting and I know Rev Birchfield and I hunted a lot together when we were young lads. We've not always been old men, you know." he informed me with a sly grin.

Opening the package, I was delighted to find a shiny new over and under double barreled 12 gauge shot gun. Wow! Nice gun. Upon close examination, I found the words carved into the stock in small, neat letters : "Moses' Rod."

"If you get the opportunity to go deer hunting, I brought you a box of double 0 buck shot. Happy hunting."

I did get to target practice a couple of times with my new gun. It held a tight pattern and I was sure we would have fresh meat for the table if I got the opportunity to go on a hunt and I got close enough to the deer. We stayed busy that winter and I didn't get the opportunity to hunt but I was getting a real education on being a pastor.

Having now delivered several messages and helping with two funerals and one wedding, Rev Birchfield informed me that the people of Twin Forks Baptist Church had been visiting recently. They had heard me preach. They had talked to Rev. Birchfield. They went home and talked to their congregation. Their old pastor, recently widowed, was retiring and moving in with daughter. They wanted me to be their pastor.

If I would accept the call, I would have five weeks to be there. They had a parsonage for me to live in. I was to let them know as soon as possible. Yes! I wanted this church. My own church. With Rev. Birchfield's recommendation, I sent my letter to them, informing them of my decision.

CHAPTER 2

ONE OF THE THINGS THAT Rev Birchfield had stressed to me in all his teachings was to rely on God for all my needs. He based his simple faith message on the Scripture about Abraham and his son Isaac. When they were preparing an altar for sacrifice, Isaac had inquired of his father, "Where is the lamb?" Abraham's simple reply, found in Gen. 22-8 was, "God will provide."

After my reply to the church had been sent, someone had asked about a single man going forth to pastor a church. "Some people don't like that. They believe their pastor should be the husband of one wife."

When I discussed this with Rev Birchfield, his simple reply was, "God will provide." "But I don't even have any prospects. All the young ladies back home who were sure I would be a fine catch when they thought I would move in with my dad in his business and have a nice, new home and a nice, big income, suddenly lost interest when they found out I was going into the ministry. When I went home for Christmas, they were glad to see me but they sure didn't give the slightest indication that they were casting their net my way."

I packed a couple of big trunks with almost everything I owned and shipped them directly to Twin Forks Baptist Church. The church held an ordination service and I was now a legal, ordained minister. I could, among other things, pastor a church, hold conference, preform a wedding and a lot of other stuff. I was a pastor!

I rounded up the remainder of my belongings, including Moses' Rod, and bid goodby to Rev. and Mrs. Birchfield and boarded the stagecoach for home. I would spend a few days with the family, then be off to Twin Fork.

We had left just as dawn was breaking and the journey was long and tiring. Several times we had stopped, taking on or discharging passengers and loading or unloading freight destined for further up the road. Finally, just before sunset, there was only the last stop left. Home. Tired and dusty and none too warm, I found myself the lone passenger.

Fully awake now and moving around inside to get warm, there was a gun shot and someone yelling for the stage to stop. A gunman just ahead was blocking the road and there was hoof beats coming behind. Without thinking or hesitation, I poked Moses' Rod out the window and let fly at the gunman's right side and his rifle. Quickly reversing my view, the other barrel was emptied at one of the approaching riders. Two new shells replaced the spent ones and the other two gunmen received a dose of buckshot.

The stage driver had taken off at the first gunshot from inside the stage. We were on a wild ride for a minute or two and then we were greeted by the sheriff and his posse. They rushed to the place of the attempted holdup and captured the four bandits.

We went on into town. The sheriff soon followed with the report that all four had suffered some damage from buckshot! I was asked to stay nearby until the Judge could be called and a trial held. This delayed my going to Twin Forks. All were found guilty and I was informed that there might be a reward for what I had done to aid the capture.

If there's anything coming, just send it to Twin Forks Baptist Church. I'm sure that they could use it. I'm their new pastor." All the paperwork was fixed up and signed. It would be paid directly to the church if there was anything.

Well, that had taken a lot of time and now there was no question of how to get to Twin Forks. No stage would be going that would make connections. Horseback thru the mountains was the only choice if I were to be there to deliver my first sermon next Sunday. And, I sure didn't want to be late. A two day ride at best.

Packing all the necessary stuff I would need, including a small axe, a coffee pot and frying pan and grub enough for more than two days as mom worried I'd be hungry, I saddled my big, black horse and Tobe and I left for Twin Forks.

After a few hours, we didn't see any sign of civilization. Moving thru the big mountains we finally toward evening headed down to where there would be people.

We were still at least 10 miles from Twin Forks, up on the headwaters that made up one side of Twin Forks. Night was coming on and it was getting mighty cold, mighty fast. I spotted a building. Some kind of shed used during roundup or perhaps an abandoned trappers dwelling. It would have to do. Opening the big door on the side, I found a stable on one side and an empty room on the other. A fireplace! Nothing fancy, but a refuge from the coming storm for both me and Tobe.

I remembered, "God will provide" and happily unsaddled Tobe, tied on his feed bag with a generous helping of oats, retrieved my small axe and went outside to attract the dead tree that was lying nearby. I tried to light a fire but the chimney wouldn't cooperate. I found a pole and dislodged the nest out of the chimney. Now it worked fine. Thank you Lord.

A lot more wood was needed. The weather had turned nasty. Now it just wasn't the cold. Sleet had started to cover everything and the wind had decided to join the fun. This was going to be a night to remember. And, darkness was fast approaching.

Hurrying inside with my third load of wood, I caught a movement out of the corner of my eye. Something or someone was in the lone bunk. I heard a sob. "What was going on? Who's there?"

"Please mister. I just wanted to get warm and leave. I saw the smoke from your fire and slipped inside. I'm freezing. Please!" Another sob.

"Just calm down. Sure you can stay and warm yourself. I've probably got enough grub with me to feed us both. Now, get up and move over to the fire."

While she was doing this, I filled the coffee pot and set it to cook by the fire. I retrieved the skillet and the meat and set about slicing meat and dropping it into the pan. As it cooked over the fire, I opened a can of beans. I poured her a cup of steaming coffee and watched as she sipped on the brew.

"Guess we'll have to share the same cup and plate as I wasn't expecting company."

I removed the meat from the fire, sat it on the small, rickety table and paused to say grace. "Help yourself. There's plenty." I gave her the plate and fork along with a generous helping of beans and meat. I began to eat with my fingers. She didn't hesitate. She seemed to inhale the food. I added wood to the fire and still it was so cold. I closed the big door and taking out a big ball of heavy twine, tied it to the post. A shutter dangled by one hinge by the open window. This got the same treatment.

Winter raged outside as it tried to hit the country a final lick before spring arrived. "Now that all that is taken care of, you and I must talk. Who are you and what are you doing here? You were sure hungry just now."

"I ran away from the orphanage. I'll never go back there again. They can't force me to return. I was supposed to leave last year when I turned 16 but the overseer's wife was ill and they asked me to stay. I agreed and everything was fine until his wife died. Then, he decided that I should become his wife or lover or whatever he wanted. He kept the pressure on until I couldn't stand it any more, so I ran away."

" I've been lost for several hours and haven't eaten since I had a small, raw potato before I went to sleep in a barn loft last night"

"Well, food we have. Shelter, such as it is, we have. We don't have enough wood to keep a big fire going all night, so we have a big problem. Staying warm. I don't know of but one thing to do. You get in the bunk and lay down." Reluctantly, she obeyed. I unrolled my bedroll and tossed her my pillow out of it. I'm a softie. I carry a pillow. Piling all the bedroll on top of her including the ground cover sheet and the saddle blanket, I asked, "How's that?"

" I suppose it's all right but what about you?" " I was afraid you were going to ask that." We don't have any choice. I'm getting in there with you."

"Oh, no you're not. That's not going to happen. Never. I promised my mother as she lay dying that I would never sleep with a man unless we we're married. No. No way."

"We have two choices. We can get under the pile of covers, keep each other warm or we can let one of us freeze to death. There's not enough wood to keep a big fire all night. We can't get outside in this and get more wood. Lay still. I mean you no harm. I'm not willing to die tonight if I can help it and I sure don't want your death on my conscience."

" I have a simple solution to our problem. Give me your right hand." At first, she didn't want to do it. Then, probably worrying where my hand might wind up if she didn't, she reluctantly gave me her cold hand. "Now, what is your full, legal name?"" Mary Ann McGuffy" she whispered.

"Do you, Mary Ann McGuffy, take this man who you now hold by his right hand to be your lawful wedded husband, to have and to hold, in sickness and in health, for richer or poorer, so long as you both shall live? The answer is, I do." I heard a sharp intake of breath and I felt her tremble. "The answer is, I do" I urged her. "I do" she whispered.

"And, do you, Joseph Edgar Hendrix take this woman you now hold by your right hand to be your lawful wedded wife, to have and to hold, in sickness and in health, for richer or poorer, so long as you both shall live? And my answer is "I do."

"I now, by the power invested in me as an ordained minister of the gospel of Jesus Christ, declare us to be husband and wife." Another gasp. "You can hush now and quit worrying. We're married. You can go to sleep."

"You can't be serious. And, pretending to be a preacher. God have mercy on both of us. He may strike us both dead."

"I told you not to worry. I assure you that I am indeed an ordained minister. I am on my way to Twin Fork to pastor the church there."

"And, it's legal to preform your own wedding service?"

"I'm not really sure how legal it is. Have you a better solution? If not, when we get to Twin Forks tomorrow, we'll ask the retiring pastor to do it again, just to make sure. We wouldn't want any one questioning us about our marriage."

"God will provide." When I said this, she remained silent and I had to wonder if she had gone to sleep, passed out from fright or what. Finally, with a sigh, she said, "Joseph Edgar Hendrix, like it or not, you now have a wife. One determined to last you a lifetime. Good night."

I felt her relax against me and in a few moments, I heard her deep breathing to indicate that sleep had overtaken her. I lay there, in awe, as what we had done began to sink in and I too drifted away.

CHAPTER 3

Twice in the night, I briefly left the bed and added a small amount of wood to the fire, just to keep it going and to keep the worst of the cold at bay. The third time, I remained up and began to build up a big fire. I fixed a fresh pot of coffee and again fed Tobe his oats.

As I was slicing the meat, Mary Ann climbed out of bed and helped herself to a hot cup of coffee. As I was putting the finishing touches on our breakfast she said "I've gotta go." "In the back of the stable. Tobe won't mind. You can't go outside in this weather."

After breakfast, everything was packed up and ready to load on Tobe. I gave her my spare pair of pants and told her to get them on and use a length of cord to hold them on. My rain slicker and toboggan completed her outfit. With saddle in place and the bedroll secured behind, Tobe was led outside and we mounted up. "Put your arms around me and put your hands in my coat pockets. I have only one pair of gloves."

The wind had died. The sleet and snow had stopped. Everything was so white it would hurt your eyes. We must have been a pretty sight. We moved at a leisure pace, not wanting to chance of injury if our horse lost his footing. The temperate began to rise. Soon it was on the plus side of zero.

Rough figuring, if we made the estimated remaining ten miles in three hours we would be fine. Turned out, a little over four hours were needed. We first saw the buildings in the distance then finally, we were there.

A cafe looked promising and we dismounted and went inside. "Hot coffee! Two steaming cups appeared and we received them with gladness. Making small talk with our waitress, the front door opened and the sheriff came in. I inquired of him if Rev. Browne was still around. "He's probably up in his room. You need to see him?"

After I explained to him who I was and why I was there, he hurriedly sent someone for the preacher. I quietly explained to him about our marriage and he said, "Write both your full names on this sheet of paper. Florence, would you and the sheriff join me in the kitchen please. Come on, you two."

Safely inside the kitchen, Rev Browne faced us and said, "You have both made your vows and your wedding is probably legal. However, to remove all doubt on the matter, unite your right hands. I now pronounce you man and wife. You may kiss the bride."

A kiss befitting my sister was exchanged and Rev Browne said, "What we do here is to remain here. I'll file the necessary paper work and you two can sign as witnesses."

Word quickly spread that the new pastor and his wife had arrived. I ask that someone go with my wife and get her some new clothes as we didn't have any of her clothes with us. She didn't have any, but I wasn't going to tell them that. Some of the church ladies captured her and they went away to do all the things that women do.

Someone of the men took Tobe to the parsonage stable and tended to him. Someone else went to the parsonage and lit the fires. I unpacked clean clothes and made my way to the barber shop for a shave, a haircut and a bath.

Rev. Browne took me around and I met several of the people. "We can't go into the church right now. School is still in session." The same building was both church and school.

Finally, late in the evening I was allowed to go back to the parsonage. When I went inside, there was this very pretty blond headed lady in a nice dress and her hair all doodied up. I did a double take! "Mary Ann? Is that you? I hardly recognize you." You look fabulous!"

She blushed a nice pink and I suppose I did too, being so bold. "What did you think you had married? A rag doll? You don't look bad yourself."

"Aw, come on in before we really mess this up." What could I do. I found the house to be filled with the wonderful aroma of supper. The women of the church were responsible for all this. We said grace and enjoyed the luxury of a wonderful meal, topped of with a big bowl of peach cobbler pie.

As we were eating, Mary Ann asked, "Should we worry about people being told about our little mess?" "Florence seems the type to keep quiet and I knew that the pastor and sheriff are lodge brothers and they won't talk."

"Lodge brothers?" she inquired. "Yep. They are both Masons. We don't have to worry about them gabbing."

"They told you this? I didn't hear anything about it." "Nope. Didn't have to be told. We just know." She let it rest there, still not entirely satisfied that I knew what I was talking about.

We discussed several things as we ate. Getting acquainted with each other. So many questions remained for both of us. I kept stealing admiring glances at her. With her hair freshly shampooed and a new dress that fit her nicely, she sure was pretty.

I finally asked, "Last night, you finally relaxed and went to sleep. How did you decide that everything was going to be all right?" She had a simple explanation. She had prayed, "Lord, help me. I'm depending on you in all this to make everything right. When you said, God will provide, I knew my prayers had been answered, weird as it seemed at the time."

So began our life. A new pastor with a new wife. You might say, this can't possibly work out. They just met. And married! Ask yourself a simple question. How long had Isaac known Rebekah before they wed? Genesis 24:67 has the answer if you care to look. When God does something, he does it right. And there was no doubt in the mind of either of us that this is exactly what had happened.

Bed time came and the newly married couple slipped into the same bed for tonight there would be no objections. In fact, there was wonder and awe and the delightful experience of really getting to know each other. No more brother sister kissing. Tonight, and for the remainder of their life, they became lovers.

Saturday morning. Another great surprise. This wife could cook. Not just throw something at the cook stove. She knew how to make a delicious meal. As they were eating, she asked, "What should I call you? As a wife, seems to me I should know. Is it Joe or Joseph or just what name do you prefer?"

"Mamma always calls me Joseph. Dad prefers to call me Joe. Sis usually calls me "Hey you" or something like that so I'll leave that up to you. Should I call you Mary Ann?"

"Mary Ann is fine and I guess I'll just wait and decide what to call you. Your sis may have the right idea" With a laugh she disappeared out the door and I went to the barn to check on Tobe. He was fine with a nice, clean stable, a rack filled with sweet smelling hay and a corral big enough to stretch out his legs and get a drink of water from the spring branch.

I wanted some time alone for prayer and sermon preparation for tomorrow but it just wasn't to be. Seems everyone in town wanted to drop by and just say "Hi" to us, shake hands and slip quietly away, only to have someone else come by just as they were leaving.

Late Saturday afternoon I finally managed to slip inside the church for the very first time. It had been changed from classroom to church in preparation for tomorrow. I rode a wild bucking horse of emotions as I stood there. I loved the church and the people. How wonderful to be their pastor. How scary the responsibilities seemed. It would be so easy to be completely overwhelmed from all this.

As I was contemplating all this, someone quietly slipped in behind me and I felt her arms go around me and she said, "God will provide. Isn't he wonderful! I have a new home, a new husband and a new church family. Life is good."

If that won't lift you up to a new level. If that doesn't set your heart to running a little faster, there's something wrong with you. I turned and gave her a big hug. "Thanks, I needed that!" Arm in arm we returned to the parsonage, ready to take on the world together.

CHAPTER 4

Early Sunday morning found Mary Ann and I stationed at the front entrance of the church, greeting everyone as they came in. Names and faces ran together. Our reception was warm and the church was filling rapidly. Everyone apparently wanted an opportunity to meet the new pastor and see what kind of preacher they had.

After the church had sung some old, familiar songs, the sheriff, who happened to also be my chief deacon, had the other deacons receive the morning offering and then introduced me as the new pastor.

After exchanging pleasantries with my chief deacon and greeting everyone, I read my scripture and began. It was more a message about my calling and my early troubles than anything else. I did reach down and stir some heart when I made the statement, "God is good – All the time." I heard a soft "amen" from Mary Ann and I noticed a tear as it slipped down her cheek.

Later she said, "I didn't realize that was going to happen. Both the tear and the "amen" had slipped out and I just couldn't stop either one." Now, stuff like that will have this young preacher walking on air!

I had received another pleasant surprise. As the church had been singing, I listened as my new wife joined right in. Her voice blended in with the others and made my pitiful attempts sound lame by comparison.

The congregation received the message with gladness and assured us that they would return and try to bring others with them. This warmed my heart to know that, so far, everything was wonderful. Little did I realize what the future had in store for me.

Our honeymoon continued, both as newly weds and as a new pastor for Twin Forks Baptist Church. A check arrived from Wells Fargo and went into the building fund. We were assured now that there was enough funds for a new building and we wouldn't have the school and church in the same building.

Two weeks. Two weeks and beginning the third. Life was wonderful. In fact, life was a dream. Then, a knock on the door. It was mid afternoon and we were now accustomed to our people dropping by all the time.

But this wasn't one of our members. This was a big, red faced man who was ready to throw a temper fit on whoever got in his way. And I was the one who was in his way.

"Where is she?" He screamed. "I demand that you return the little runaway hussy to me at once. I'm going to teach her a lesson she will never forget. Where is she? They told me that I would find the ungrateful child here."

Stepping out on the porch, I closed the door behind me. "Just who are you and who is it you're looking for?" I asked as calmly as I could, even though I felt my throat going dry and felt a tremble in my hand. I was scared. I was mad. To say that I was upset wouldn't do my feelings justice.

"Mary Ann McGuffy, that's who. Send her out here and right now. If you don't, I'm calling the sheriff."

"That won't be necessary for you to do that. I'll call the sheriff myself." I had spotted one of my members walking down the street and called, "Frank,can you ask the sheriff to come over here. We need him. Now." Frank moved quickly down the street and moments later the sheriff walked up to the porch.

"What seems to be the problem?" the sheriff asked.

"I am Solomon Jones. I am in charge of the orphanage over at Big Bear. A child from the orphanage has run away and I've followed her trail to here. I demand that she be returned to my care at once."

"Who is this child and how old is she?" the sheriff inquired.

"As I have already told this buffoon standing here, her name is Mary Ann McGuffy and she's a 13 year old waif who would lie about anything and steal the coins from a dead man's eyes. I demand that she be returned to me at once. I am totally responsible for her until she turns 16."

I was in shock. This was my wife he was talking about. My greatest desire right now was to see how hard I could drive my fist into his loud mouth. Had it not been for the sheriff standing there, I'm sure I would have tried violence on this stranger. I loved this woman. I was just beginning to realize how much that she meant to me.

"Well, Mr. Solomon Jones, I am the sheriff. My name is John Simmons. What we are going to do is call a special meeting at the church in one hour.

Meanwhile, I suggest you go somewhere and cool off. Get a cup of coffee down town. Meet us at the church in one hour and don't be late.

We'll settle this thing then and there. If you're not there, I'm coming after you."

He didn't like the turn of events. He didn't like it at all. He spent the next hour stewing in his own mad fit. He was in front of the church, stomping and huffing and puffing. Wasn't doing him a bit of good. School hadn't been dismissed for the day. Fifteen minutes before the scheduled meeting, children came pouring out of the building.

Well, I discovered, as soon as the meeting started, our sheriff sure had a real talent for drama. There was several of the leading business men of Twin Forks right up front. Several of them I recognized as part of the church body as well as members of the local Masonic Lodge. He invited Mr. Solomon Jones to come to the front and state his case.

He didn't dare use the vile language he had so easily thrown around, we being now in the Lords house. He did, however spew forth his venom about my beloved until I wanted desperately to choke the crap out of him.

The sheriff then called for several women to come forth. Included in the half dozen females was my beloved wife, Florence from the cafe and the sheriff's perky thirteen year old red headed daughter. Freckled faced and wearing pigtails, with a figure like a broom handle, she was quiet a contrast.

"Now sir, we here are aware of one thirteen year old present. Would you please see if the female you seek is present here today. We have all heard your description of your thirteen year old."

The room became deadly quiet. No one moved. Solomon Jones began to fidget and huff and puff. "Let me introduce these ladies to you. This is the mayor's wife. This lady is married to our banker. This is Florence who owns and runs the local cafe, this is our pastor's wife and this is my wife and daughter, who just happens to be thirteen.

Now, I must ask you sir, do you see this thirteen year old waif you are seeking?"

"Well? I'm waiting for your answer. Is there anyone present here who fits the description you gave us?" Finally, he muttered "No" and bowed his head. "Speak up Mr. Jones. We want everyone here to hear you." Finally, he looked up, shook his head and declared, "No. I guess I was mistaken."

"Well then, I believe that you owe Rev. Hendrix an apology for the things that you said to him earlier today. If you'll do that, we will bring this meeting to a close and be on our way." Then he asked that Mary Ann and I both come and stand directly in front of Solomon Jones. "He has something to say to both of you." the sheriff announced.

For all his bluster and name calling earlier, he sure had a hard time finding the words. He did finally mummer "I'm sorry." After both Mary Ann and I agreed to accept his apology the sheriff announced that this meeting was over and everyone was dismissed with his thanks.

Mary Jo, the sheriff's fiery red headed wife, who was also our school marm, said, "Imagine trying to say Mary Ann was only thirteen. The scoundrel. He can't even tell a believable lie."

"I don't care if she's thirteen or ten, she's my wife, I love her and I'm keeping her!" There was no argument on that one, only some very big smiles and several pats on the back. Our life was back on track, at least for now.

CHAPTER 5

BACK TO NORMAL. REALLY? WHAT is considered normal for a pastor, I began to wonder. Go over, again, the plans for the new church building. I wanted it to have room for a Sunday school department. That's something that they had never had and never considered until now.

Then, I found that there were two people that had joined the church over the winter. They had never been baptized and I was expected to preform this duty as soon as it was warm enough.

Another young couple, explaining to me that they were newly engaged, wanted to be married in the new church building, which was a fine church on paper but that's where it was right now, on paper. They wanted us to hurry!

I would be expected to hold a revival meeting come fall. "When the corn is ripe in the garden and just right for eating, it's revival time." A simple enough rule. Gardens were just now being plowed and prepared for planting and already future church plans relied on the corn being ripe. And naturally, they all expected this to be done in the new church building.

I sent my dad a lengthy letter, explaining all about the new church building. Since this was somewhat in his line of business, he sent two experienced carpenters who were also pretty good rock masons. We had the funds available to purchase materials. Three days were spent on the old church building, changing it into a "school only" building.

The plans were in hand. The materials arrived and everyone set to work with an enthusiasm that was hard to believe. I had heard of house raisings and barn raisings but this was a church raising. Everyone pitched in. In an amazing short time, where there had been an empty lot there now stood a building. There was two extra rooms for classes. Kids church, they named it. And, there was even a small room designated "Pastor's study."

Church services were hard to handle for a couple of weeks. The old building had been changed and the new one wasn't ready. Services were held one Sunday out under the big oak tree in the new building's yard.

And this was just the good stuff going on.

Some people apparently didn't want a new church building. This is where mamma and daddy went to church. This is where we have always gone to church and we don't see any reason to change anything. Didn't matter that the old building was getting crowded and the school really needed the changes that were made to make it more "school friendly."

I didn't recall these people being at church since I had been there. It hadn't been very many weeks, but still, seems I would have met them before. They refused to come to the new church. "It ain't right." Somehow the church, the new pastor and God himself survived without their help.

That spring, on the 30th of May, Mary Ann celebrated her 18th birthday. I had learned that her father had been a huge Scotch Irish man with a heart of gold. Unfortunately, while she was still a small child, he had been killed in an accident. Her widowed mother, a blonde from Sweden, had a hard struggle raising her only child. Sickness had overcome her and when she passed away, Mary Ann had ended up in the orphanage.

Apparently, when Solomon Jones had tried to pass off Mary Ann off as being only 13 years old, the seed had been planted in the mind of Mary Jo that here was a young lady who needed a mother figure and she was just the one God had in mind for this task. I could have not been more pleased. Imagine this young, tall blonde and this short, fiery red head as they bonded with a real 13 year old to keep them both on their toes.

That fall when school started again, instead of having one classroom and one teacher for everyone, the "new" school house had expanded and now there were three separate rooms. In addition to all my duties as pastor, I was also asked to teach the oldest group of children. I had enough "schoolin'" before my call into the ministry to make this possible. Mary Ann, with all her experience with children at the orphanage was asked to teach the youngest.

Tobe and I spent quiet a bit of time together as I traveled to visit with our church members scattered over the country which included both farms and cattle ranches. A small buggy, the property of the church, was used when both Mary Ann and I made a visit. Since we were now also teachers, we informed all the children about all the changes and when the opening of school was.

Late one evening, just before bedtime and well after supper, there came a knock on the parsonage door. A soft tap, tap and before I could get the door open, a loud pounding and someone yelling, "Hey! Open up!"

When I opened the door, I was greeted by a man with bloodshot eyes and a breath that bore testimony that somewhere there was a freshly emptied whiskey bottle. "Preacher, you got to help me." I managed to guide him to a chair in the dining room. He sat at the table and began to cry. If you have ever had experience with a crying drunk, you can appreciate what we faced.

On and on he rambled. He talked about being lost and needing prayer. I had no doubt about that, but in his present condition, I wondered how much we could really accomplish and how much he would even remember, come tomorrow.

Finally, when it became apparent that this wasn't going anywhere, Mary Ann slipped out the back door and hurried to find the sheriff. I didn't like the idea of her out, alone at night, but what else could we do? Sit up all night with a crying drunk, that's what.

John came in quietly and escorted our visitor away, going only after I assured him that I would come get him out in the morning. Seems that he had been in the habit of doing this on occasion. He didn't drink all the time. But, when he did, he went all out. Then, at the height of his fling with white lightning, he would end up at the parsonage for a good cry. John would come and get him and let him sleep it off.

Yep. Just a typical summer for a new pastor and his wife. That is, until the stranger showed up in town. A stranger looking for trouble.

CHAPTER 6

EARLY THE NEXT MORNING, I arrived at the jail. "Come on out, Jason Fudge. This is Rev. Hendrix. He insists that he be allowed to take you over to the restaurant and let Florence feed you a big breakfast."

"What? Rev. Browne never did that. I'm sorry preacher. I truly am. Just let me go sheriff and I'll be on my way. I don't want to be any bother."

With a smile I told him, "This ain't no bother, this is a pleasure. I told you that I would be to get you this morning. Come on. Florence is expecting us. After what you did last night, don't disappoint me now."

We had no more than seated ourselves when Mary Ann came in and joined us. Florence piled our plates high with country cured ham, hot biscuits with cream gravy. Steaming hot mugs of coffee and a side order of stewed apples.

After asking God's blessings on us and the food, we began to eat.

Jason didn't have a lot to say this morning. I asked him to please drop by the parsonage any time for a visit and to come to church services. He tried to explain to me that he wasn't good enough, because of what he had done. I explained to him that God could take care of all that and I would be happy to discuss it with him at any time.

"Let's walk over to sheriff Simmons house. I need to talk to Mary Jo about some of the things we will be doing when school starts. I'm so excited. I've been praying that I'll be able to do this job right." Since I had a question or two myself, I quickly agreed to go with her.

"There he is! There's that man who claims to be a preacher. He's the one who shot my brother and probably left him a cripple for life. If you people knew what manner of man you were getting, he wouldn't be here. He's not fit to be called a Christian. He can't be a God called preacher."

All this was yelled at us. He was near the saloon and I would suppose he had been inside, just waiting for his opportunity to spew his hatred out for the entire town to hear. If that was his plan, it had certainly succeeded.

I felt Mary Ann stiffen. "Just who are you and what are you talking about? This is the Pastor of Twin Forks Baptist Church and he's also my husband. I don't know you and I certainly don't know what you're talking about."

"Ask him. He's the one who shot my brother. I'm Elmer Carthage and my brother Henry is crippled and will never be able to work again. Your husband did the shooting and that sawbones who gained all his skills trying to put those rebel soldiers back together several years ago, finished the job."

With that, he whirled and mounted his horse. "I'll be around. I want every one to know what he's done to Henry." With that, he and his horse galloped out of town.

To say that I was stunned was putting it mildly. I knew who Henry Carthage was. Of course I knew. He was one of the outlaws that had been attempting the stage holdup when I opened up with Moses' Rod. A liberal dose of double 0 buckshot applied to the right hand, arm and shoulder would have that effect and I believed that he was probably the one in front.

I hadn't known the names until the trial, but I remembered. And now I was to be harassed and prosecuted for what I had done. It wasn't for the generous reward money. It had all gone into the building fund. I figured that when any one used a firearm to rob someone else that, if anything happened to them while they were breaking the law, they were paid for. In my mind, justice had been served thru my use of Moses' Rod.

Also, for the first time ever, I discovered that Mary Ann had a temper. We went on to the sheriff's house. She told Mary Jo, "That renegade jumped on my husband. I wanted to claw his eyes out. I remembered that I'm a preacher's wife and that alone was all that held me back." She was still shaking.

Now, I had the task of explaining to my wife and Mrs. Simmons just what had happened and what Elmer Carthage had been talking about. "And you haven't shared this with your wife? It happened just before you arrived here, is that correct?"

"Yes, that's right."

"Now, tell me something. Why did she not know? How long did you two know each other before you married?

Trying to look really, really serious, I scratched my chin as if in deep thought. "Well, I'm sure it was over an hour. Wasn't quiet two. I'd say it was probably 90 minutes, wouldn't you say that is correct honey?"

"No. I don't think it was that long. It was right after supper that night. We told John about it the next day but I don't believe we discussed the time frame." This was my wife, being very serious.

John came in about that time, so he had to be told all about the threat. "I checked up on where that reward money for the church came from and why the church was getting it. "I knew most of the details on that." When his wife questioned him about our marriage his simple reply, "Yep. If I remember correctly, ninety minutes sounds about right, give or take a few minutes."

Mary Jo was beside herself. "Ninety minutes. And I can see that you two are deeply in love. This can't be. I mean, seriously. John and I had known each other a long time. We were engaged for three months and people talked about us because we got married so quick."

"When God does something, you don't question Him. You simply believe that He knows what He's doing. When the scriptures say, God will provide, we believed that what happened and what we were doing was God's will and so far everything has been just wonderful" With these and many other words we convinced poor Mary Jo that what we had told her was true – All of it.

Now it became apparent that when I went out to call on our church members or potential church members, with the threats of Elmer Carthage hanging over my head, Moses' Rod would ride in the buggy with me. I didn't like the idea of having to carry a gun. Neither did I want to face a man filled with vengeance with no protection.

CHAPTER 7

I FRETTED OVER THIS ALL week. Who wouldn't worry? After all, I was being harassed by this man. I prayed for guidance. "Why me, Lord? What had I done to deserve this? What should I do?" Yet, I could come up with no solution.

Friday evening, as Mary Ann and I were enjoying a quiet meal together at home, God revealed several things to me while I sat there, really stunned in my own mind by what happened. I had heard Rev Birchfield say something about "When we were called to pastor this church" and I couldn't quiet get it in my mind what he was talking about. Mrs Birchfield did not preach and yet he referred to the job of pastor as "we."

This night, my eyes were opened and I embraced the "we" in being a pastor to the people of Twin Forks.

"I know how you have worried about this" she began. 'I have been reading God's word and praying about this. The simple solution, I believe, is to heap coals of fire on his head."

"Wow! Great thought. How do we get him to sit still while we pile all those coals of fire on his head? Boy. I'll bet that's going to hurt!" I was half serious and full of questions.

"In Romans, chapter 12, verses 19 and 20, Paul talks about this very thing. If we follow these directions, I see no reason that it wouldn't work." By the way, not only does this scripture teach that this is the way to heap hot coals on our enemies head, it also says that God will hand out the punishment."

Plans were made. After supper, we hurried down to the cafe. Florence was informed of our plan. I gave her enough money for several meals. If and when Elmer Carthage came in for a meal, he was to be served and when he left and attempted to pay, he was to be told "Your meal has been paid for. You may come in at any time and eat. It's all been taken care of by someone who cares. He said you were a presistant man and that you loved your brother very much."

At Sunday morning services I told them about his love for his brother and requested that all members of the church lift him up in prayer. There was a murmur that passed thru the congregation. Then, they all agreed to do this. God's spirit moved thru all of us for the remainder of the services. At the invitation, a young man came forward and with joy did receive Jesus as his personal savior. While we were rejoicing over this, his parents came forward and ask that all three of them be allowed to join our church.

I felt as though God and I were now on the same page together. I had been wondering around but my wonderful wife had brought me back to the proper path. God hadn't moved. He was right there all the time.

Tuesday found Elmer Carthage back in town. He ended up eating at Florence's cafe. He was told his meal was paid for and, with a smirk, he left. After spewing out his hatred around town for a while, he left. Friday was a repeat of Tuesday. Another week. Two more free meals and more hatred spread to anyone he could get to listen, mostly down at the local saloon.

Finally, on the third week, I suppose it was beginning to play on his mind and he was told, "Yes. It's all paid for. The gentleman who paid said you were a very presistant man and that you evidently loved your brother very much. He was apparently satisfied. He left without further questions. Twice more he availed himself of the free meal, coming back every day. Then he was told, "The gentleman who has been paying for all your meals has also requested that the entire congregation of Twin Forks Baptist Church remember you in their prayers every day."

"Boy, I bet that really put that smart Alec preacher in his place." "Why no. Didn't you know? Rev Hendrix himself was the one who did all this for you. He's the one who has been bragging on you, requesting prayer for you and paying for all your meals here. Didn't you know?"

Well, I suppose it must have been all those coals of fire that caused him to turn so red in the face, splutter about in a terrible manner, then turn and hurry out of the cafe and out of town. Two weeks later, late one afternoon a dirty and haggard Elmer Carthage knocked timidly on our front door. He stood on the porch, hat in hand and with downcast eyes, begged for forgiveness. " I ain't been able to sleep or rest after I found out what you had done for me. I know that God won't forgive me unless I have your forgiveness first. Please! Forgive me."

"Sure. I forgive you. Now, go ask God. He will, too."

I found out something else right there. Not only is it a great relief to have someone to agree to forgive you for something, it's good for the one doing the forgiving, too. Double blessings!!

Some time later that first summer, I was reading about Jesus, as he was right in the middle of giving his life, shedding his lifeblood for the sins of all, he was able to pray for those very ones doing all this, "Forgive them Father for they know not what they do."

If he could do this, surely I could forgive a man who was merely talking bad about me. More light. More wisdom.

Then, in the middle of summer, after the crops had been planted and before it was time to harvest them, the ladies of the church decided we should have a bible school for all the children that they could round up. Wasn't necessary that their parents were a member of the church. If they were old enough to be left by themselves and young enough not to be considered an adult, they were invited.

One of the things that had inspired them, as if they needed anything to encourage them, a new piano had arrived. There had been enough money left over from building the church to pay for it. Now, after weeks of waiting, it had arrived and, don't you know, these ladies wanted everyone to see and hear it.

The children learned bible verses. They played games. They ate home made cookies and cupcakes. They sang songs as Mrs. Loretta, the postmaster's wife, played the new piano for them. Mary Ann and I were right in the middle of everything. Saturday evening was the big final! All family and friends were expected to be there.

Friday evening, I delivered the simple message of salvation and, at the invitation, five young people came forward. Two were from our church family. Two were from the Methodist church on the other end of town which was just starting up and one child I had no idea about. But God knew her and there was no doubt, she was a new, born again Christian!!

What a wonderful time. What a great summer. And, I found a new brother in Christ. I went over to the south side of town to see the Methodist minister to inform him of the two new converts for his church and invite him to come to Bible School Graduation.

CHAPTER 8

I found Rev. Johnson to be a delightful man who was just as enthusiastic about the Lord's work as I was and who was delighted about his new converts. Homer, as I was instructed to call him, was a short, heavy individual.

Summer passed all too quickly. One of the big things around Twin Forks was the combination of fishing tournament and fish fry, Florence donated the use of her cafe for the afternoon and evening. If no one caught any cooking size fish, it would have been bad. No worries. Fresh fish from both forks and the main stream were cleaned and cooked. This was a fundraiser for the expenses of running the town government and the Mayor declared it a huge success.

My second career was suddenly here. School opened and Mary Ann made sure we were there early to greet all the children. A new school building and two new teachers! Mary Jo was a bundle of energy, trying to be everywhere at once.

All the children had to be registered. Most had been in school last year but there we re some whose parents had moved in over the summer.

And then, there were the little ones, entering school for the first time. Mary Ann soon had her hands full with eight students, from beginners thru age eight.

Mary Jo had all the middle sized children and that left the big kids to me. Four boys and two girls. I had ordered new study material for my class. Once again, Mom and Dad had come thru. They had found the latest books, paid for them and shipped them to Twin Forks.

Then, just as everything was beginning to settle down at school, it was time for harvest break and fall revival at the church. Rev Birchfield had been invited to help with the preaching and I was happy to see my mentor and once again hear him as he opened God's word and moved us with a spirit filled message.

Rev Johnson was there every night with his support of God's work. People that I hadn't met before or, if I had, I didn't remember them, came to the services.

New converts! Re-dedications! Others who were Christians but not church members, came forward. And, I got a special blessing. Little Susan, who had been saved at Bible school, had requested prayer for her parents.

They didn't come to revival with her. That is, they didn't show up until the last night. When the invitation was given, Susan came down the aisle with a parent in each hand.

Mr. and Mrs. Elmer Carthage, Susan's parents, with tears in their eyes, knelt for prayer and gladly received Christ as savior.

"A child shall lead them" came to mind. This wonderful youngster had prayed for them ever since bible school. God heard and answered. The man who had started out as my enemy had become my brother in Christ!

When we closed the revival, we had a big "Dinner on the ground" service after Sunday morning preaching, then, in mid afternoon, everyone gathered at the Twin Forks swimming hole for the Baptizing services.

Then, Monday morning, it was back to school. Where did all the time go?

CHAPTER 9

Six big children. No problems, right? Wrong. I was soon to discover the error of my thinking. The four boys had a choice. Attend school or do hard labor at their farm or ranch. Both girls parents had reluctantly allowed them to enroll. Women didn't need so much learning, did they?

On the other hand, not one of my students wanted to cause trouble and have me talk to their parents since, if that happened, their school days would be over.

The girls wanted to learn. The boys wanted to get out of all that hard work, so they had to put forth some kind of effort. I didn't want to lose any of them so it was up to me to keep everything interesting and informative enough to keep everything going.

For reading, we had the Bible, some poetry and some drama in the form of plays. These came from my parents. Then, we had geography and history and current events. For this, we had a subscription to a paper from back east. Usually, our paper was only a couple of weeks old when it arrived, so we were well informed. This paper is expensive, but I figure it's money well spent.

While school was out for harvest break and revival, an idea came to me. I had been trying to think of something to really grab the interest of the entire class.

"Do you remember our first meal together?"

I asked Mary Ann one night at the supper table. "Sure I do. Country cured ham and a can of beans."

"Well, I've been thinking. What if we had a cannery right here in Twin Forks. Do you suppose we could get the small farmers around here to grow enough extra vegetables to support a cannery? Let's ask Florence what canned food she buys for the cafe and we can check with Gus and see what he sells at the store."

"We might be able to use a case or two here when the church has one of those fellowship meals. I like the idea." said Mary Ann. "But, that is going to cost a lot of money. Where will that come from? And, who will run it?"

Dad and Mom are coming for a visit during the Thanksgiving holidays. "I'm hoping that they will find the idea to be a good one and will help with the financial end. As for management, my class at school needs a real project. I believe that this could be it."

Cool weather, Thanksgiving, Dad and Mom and all the excitement of having a few days off. Then, there was the turkey shoot, sponsored by the lodge, to raise money for their projects.

I invited all four of my school boys to the contest and agreed to let each one have a couple of turns with Moses' Rod. All four won a prize that day so they were pleased as punch with having the opportunity to shoot Moses' Rod.

And I would have won the main prize, a big turkey, if my dad hadn't been there. Still, I couldn't complain since this would be our Thanksgiving bird.

Dad and Mom now had the opportunity to really get acquainted with their new daughter in law. It was no surprise to me how they felt about her. She was a real jewel. Mary Ann, however, was so overwhelmed that she could scarcely contain herself. "Your Dad and Mom are so wonderful. I love them already."

"Guess they know a good thing when they see it! Just proves once again, God knows what he's doing. He gave them a wonderful daughter in law!" I got a big hug and kiss for that remark.

CHAPTER 10

It was a two way street. Mom and Mary Ann had cooked the Thanksgiving meal together. After asking the blessing and while we were eating, Mom quietly said, "Son, you sure have a wonderful wife. I know that we are already bonding and she's like another daughter to me."

As Mary Ann blushed, Dad added a hearty "Amen" and the blush deepened. With tears of joy, Mary Ann Hugged them both. "God is good – All the time" I beamed. I knew that this Thanksgiving was surely the best one ever for me.

When Mary Ann and I explained our idea about a cannery here at Twin Forks, they were just as excited about the idea as we were. "For it to be successful, it must have the support of the entire town and the surrounding farms. If you two can get this together, we will support it 100%, we were told.

I knew that my parents were well off and that the money would be there when the time came. It would be set us as a co-orperation with stock and everything. Now, all I had to do was sell the idea to everyone else.

Some thought it was a wonderful idea and some took a "Wait and see" attitude but no one said no. Enough of the small farmers around agreed to grow extra vegetables and Gus agreed to sell them in his store and Florence could use quiet a bit in the cafe.

All the paper work that was involved. I insisted that the entire class be totally involved in this. It was a great educational experience, not only for them, but for their teacher as well.

The Mayor, who was also a lawyer, was brought in. With his help, articles of Incorporation were drawn up. Twin Forks cannery became a reality, at least on paper. Shares of stock were printed and ready for sale. The Mayor agreed to take shares of stock to cover his bill. There were two classes of stock, voting and non voting. The voting stock would be limited and be held mostly by the officers of the corporation.

Officers were elected and every student in my class had an office. Then, contracts were drawn, with the local small farmers agreeing to grow the crops and the cannery agreeing to purchase them.

A huge loan was made to the company. It was backed and fully guaranteed by my Dad's company. A new building. Canning equipment was ordered. And supplies,

In the spring, Dad and Mom thought it would be almost mandatory that some of us visit another cannery and learn what we could about their operations. Arrangements were made. Mary Ann and I, along with six pupils. Officers of our company, boarded a southbound stage, an extra run with no additional passengers, but with freight and mail. Then, we were so crowded that the boys had to take turns, two inside and two on top.

After many hours, we finally arrived at a town that was on the railroad. There, we boarded the train for our destination, still many miles away. This was the first trip for everyone that covered this much distance and I was the only one who had ridden on a train, so you can imagine the excitement.

Finally, bone weary, we arrived at our destination. A boarding house had agreed to have room and board ready for all of us, so with thankful hearts we found our beds and were asleep in no time. We didn't awaken until late the next morning. Well, late for us. Breakfast was ready when we came down stairs.

Our host was a jolly sort and his wife was a wonderful cook. These two weeks were going to be an exciting time. We were all ready to tackle the task at hand.

CHAPTER 11

As we were enjoying that first breakfast, our host brought up the subject of something that was happening in Washington. All my students joined right in. They were well informed, thanks to our newspaper reading and were able to offer some well thought out arguments, both pro and con. This brought a real pleasure to their teacher and I could see that our host was impressed.

As we were getting dressed to go out to the cannery, I remarked to Mary Ann, "I like our host. He seems to be a well informed individual. Also, since he is a lodge brother, I'm sure we can trust him to treat everyone right."

"Well, I know that he didn't tell you. I was with you all the time, yet, somehow, you know."

"Trust me, I know. Let's get our crew together and see if we can find the cannery. I don't believe it's very far. We can walk it easily from here."

Upon arrival, we were escorted inside by one of the workers. Mary Ann took the girls to the office where all the paperwork was handled.

The boys and I were led to the cannery its self where all the food was processed and canned. For several days, in great detail, we were shown every aspect of the workings of this cannery.

One of the bosses was taking us on this educational adventure and two note pads in the hands of four young men were rapidly filling up. I had quit thinking of them as boys and started to remind myself that they were, indeed, young men.

Also, I was soon to discover that there was a warehouse that still had can goods available for shipping and that orders were shipped out at least once a week.

Since fresh vegetables were not in season, in order for us to observe the actual processing of food and the canning process, several kettles of dried beans were processed. Several hours of pinto beans slowly cooking with a chunk of streaked "middlin'" meat sure stirred our taste buds. Instead of waiting hours, just heat and eat cans of beans.

We watched as the canning process took place and were impressed with the number of cans. They were left to cool, labels were attached to each can and then two dozen cans to a case, they were sent to the warehouse to await shipment.

One incident that was sure to remain in our memories of this trip had nothing to do with the cannery. We had decided to go "Out on the town" for an evening meal on Saturday night.

We found a nice cafe. The food was good and we enjoyed the meal. Upon leaving, a man made some crude remarks to the women folks.

When I called his hand on it and demanded an apology, he instead gave a smirk, stepped up and took a swing at me.

Big mistake. I was an ordained minister, a man of God. Also, growing up and working around the men that my dad's company employed, I had learned a thing or two about fighting. Oh yeah, and I was on the boxing team at school and had won my division the final two years. As I said, this young lad didn't know what he had gotten into.

As his roundhouse right, which he was sure would separate my head from my body, whistled harmlessly past my nose, my solid right jab caught him in the gut. This took the wind out of his sails. He wasn't satisfied, however. With a curse, he rushed me. Stepping inside, a bone jarring left to the end of his nose brought blood.

A solid one two followed and he went down, where he stayed. End of fight.

CHAPTER 12

I GOT TEASED BY THE young men as we made our way back to our rooming house and I caught an admiring glance or two from the two young ladies.

Later, at breakfast the next morning, it was mentioned again. When the description was given our host, he said, "I know exactly who you are talking about. He's a loud mouth bully. Everyone is afraid of him. First time I can remember anyone getting the best of him."

"I am a peace loving man. I didn't ask for trouble. However, I couldn't let one of our young ladies be insulted and simply stand by and do nothing. Christians are supposed to be gentle as lambs. Yet, Jesus drove the money changers from the temple. Some things you can't overlook."

We attended the local church with our host and his wife. A restful afternoon and night brought us back to the cannery for final instructions.

The size of the building, it's layout and the size of the warehouse were covered in detail. Heat for the frigid winter was another thing, No one would want canned food that had been frozen while in storage. It wasn't necessary to keep it hot or anything, just keep everything above freezing.

Then, the long, weary journey back to Twin Forks. The train ride wasn't nearly as exciting going back as it had been coming east. Sleep was the order this time and we arrived at the depot much rested and ready for our stage ride back home.

We had several notebooks crammed with notes. Plans had already been drawn for the buildings and materials were arriving as we came home. Dad had sent a work crew. Several local men were added to assist and things went well.

Some changes were made in the plans, as suggested by our business trip. The equipment arrived and was installed. Labels for the cans proudly proclaimed, "a product of Twin Forks" and bundles that identified what was inside.

Last summer, I had all I could do. I stayed busy the entire summer. Everything we did last summer was scheduled to be repeated this summer. Well, not really. I wouldn't have to do the wedding over, but you get the picture.

This summer, instead of a new church building, there was the new building for the cannery, the warehouse for the cannery, workers to hire and train for the cannery. And, all my many extra things as a pastor.

I sent Dad and Mom a rather lengthy letter describing what we had accomplished already and what we expected to do this summer. I did mention, over on page two, that they would become grandparents before the summer was out.

It was becoming harder and harder to hide what was obvious. When Mary Jo found out for sure, she was just like a mother hen with a baby chick. I knew then that my wife was in good hands.

The closer it came to opening time, I worried that my four young pupils might not be able to handle everything. I believed the girls could handle the office work. I contacted Matthew Gibbons, who had been so helpful to us on our educational journey to the other cannery, He agreed to come and help us thru our first season,

Then, there was Jason Fudge. You remember him. The town drunk, I suppose. Harmless. Usually sober. But, when he tied one on, he could be a real pain. He was still around, doing his thing.

I guess some things never change.

CHAPTER 13

WHEN MATTHEW ARRIVED, HE SUGGESTED that we cook up a mess of pinto beans and can them, just to make sure everything worked right.

Did you know that you could purchase dried beans in 50 pound bags? I didn't either. But, that's the way things are done. So we ordered in some beans and canned our first product, ever.

The beans turned out fine. I guess we got carried away with what we were doing. Can you imagine how many cans of pinto beans you can get from 200 pounds of dried beans? Believe me, it's a lot of canned beans.

Right away, a salesman was hired and he was sent out with a case of beans, 24 cans to the case. His instructions were, give one can as a free sample to stores and cafes. Give them a list of what we expected to have available and at what date. Invite them to order the beans right away and the other products as they became available.

He soon returned with a handful of orders and picked up another 2 cases and headed off in a different direction. Twin Forks cannery was in business! Bring in the new crops.

Dad, always thinking and being an astute business man with a lot invested in our cannery, sent over a cost accountant. He studied the overall picture. I didn't realize things could be so complicated. He came up with a new price list for each product to give us a reasonable profit.

The new crops ripened. They were harvested and processed. We had a lot more than I expected. A lot more. Evidently, everyone wanted to be the highest producer and we were flooded.

Just in time, our salesman returned with great news. He had secured a contract with state prison. Cases of gallon size cans were soon on their way. Our cannery was a success.

Another thing was happening. At first, no one noticed. When Matthew Gibbons came to town, a furnished apartment was rented for three months for him. Now, being a single man and a hard worker, what do you suppose he did? Yep. Three meals every day. Florence had a new, permanent customer. If good food is the way to a man's heart, Florence had the key.

When Matt and Florence came to church together and sat together, somehow we began to get the idea that this middle age couple just might become a permanent twosome.

Don't think that everything was going peachy good. It wasn't. I seemed to be working twice as hard as I had last summer and I wasn't gaining on anything. I had pulled away from the cannery and let all the others run things. I had a church to pastor. That was my first priority.

My visitation was down. Mary Ann had to stop going out with me so much and I didn't really want to get that far away from her. Delivery time was drawing closer and closer. Mary Jo kept a close eye on her and my Mom decided that she should be here for the great event so she came to stay with us.

I was quietly evicted early each morning. And, I didn't feel really comfortable being around three women all day. So, I worked. I worked hard.

Our church had many more members than when I arrived. Yet, attendance didn't pick up that much.

I worried. I fretted. I missed the council of my wife.

I talked to my Methodist pastor friend. He was experiencing the same problem. Low attendance. We prayed together for God's guidance in this.

CHAPTER 14

Different sermons serve different purposes. Not all sermons are fire and brimstone, revival meeting sermons. Some are to educate the flock. To get to know God better. To get to know what His will is for each of us. To stir each of his children to do His will with joy.

I remember one such sermon. When I read my text, Luke 2:10 "And the angel said unto them, Fear not: for, behold, I bring you good tidings of great joy, which shall be to all people."

A Christmas message? In the very middle of summer? Surely, our punching preacher is slipping. Becoming a new father any day now is getting to him. I'm sure those thoughts were going thru their minds.

But, they were wrong. It wasn't a Christmas message. The key to this message was, "I bring you good tidings of great joy!"

Happiness and joy are the same thing, isn't it? Surely many believed that when I started that morning. Hopefully, they saw the difference as I delivered God's message.

Happiness is based on outward things. Happy with that wonderful meal you just enjoyed. Happy to see someone you hadn't seen for quiet some time. Happy to get the day off to go fishing or hunting or countless other things. Happiness is like the weather. It can change at any time. And, like that great meal you ate, it won't last.

Joy, on the other hand, comes from inside. It's not something that can come and go so easily as happiness. Good tidings of what? Yep. The angel had it exactly right, "Great joy!"

It was a message of great joy as the world was to see Jesus for the first time. Now, here was truly a great joy. Everlasting joy!

In closing, you can receive this great joy if you will receive this same Jesus as your personal savior. I just thought, Wow! This is good stuff. Just think, God is good - - All the time!

One reason I can remember this message so vividly? Simple. As I was shaking hands with the departing congregation, someone rushed up to me and said, "Mary Ann is in labor!"

Now, I have had some exciting things happen to me up to this point in my life. Nothing compared to this.

I quickly greeted the remainder of the flock and hurried home. I was met at the door by my mother. Mary Jo is with your wife. She's fine. You can't go in there now.

"And, why not? I'm her husband." My voice came out somewhere between a whine and a quiver. This robust, manly preacher with a voice that would fill a church from corner to corner, could scarcely speak. Good thing no one asked me what my name was. I probably couldn't have told them.

"You just can't. That's why. It just isn't proper. Now, go away. We'll let you know when it's over. Mary Jo is with her and the doctor is coming." This was my loving Mother. My own Mother. And she talked down to me as if I were a small child. "Just leave."

"God, have mercy on us all" I thought. Being dismissed from my own home. By my own Mother. How could she do such a thing? I was already a nervous wreck and now this.

I was a pastor of the church. I was a teetotaler. I hadn't touched corn whiskey except that one time and I had swore that was my first and last.

Good thing, too. Otherwise, I would be tempted to go out and get roaring drunk.

I was out of there. I went to the porch and sat down. I got up. I walked back and forth on the porch. I sat on the steps. I went to the barn and checked on Tobe. I talked to him, He seemed to understand. He didn't interrupt me or anything. I poured my heart out to that horse.

I went back to the porch. The doctor came. Seems that everything was fine. He came outside and we talked. I heard Mary Ann Yowl. The doctor went back inside. I paced the porch. I prayed. I prayed as I had never prayed in my life.

Beads of sweat kept forming on my brow. My shirt was beginning to show signs of water seeping thru. Was it really THIS hot? The thermometer apparently lied. It can't be right.

We hear stories about how much Mothers go thru with to bring a child into this world. I have no doubt that this is true. I could hear Mary Ann inside the bedroom. If I had the slightest doubt before, that was all erased now.

However, let me assure all you ladies, becoming a new Dad is no piece of cake either. I walked for miles that afternoon. Tobe and I had several visits. For weeks this went on, months even. Finally, just before dark, Mom came out and informed me that she had a new grandson!

"That means, I'm a father! How is Mary Ann and is the baby all right? Can I go in now?" Relief came over me like a refreshing rain in the spring as Mom assured me that both Mother and son were fine and that shortly I would be allowed inside. "Just as soon as possible! TELL THEM TO HURRY!"

CHAPTER 15

GABRIEL OLIVER HENDRIX. OUR NEW son! The smile on the face of Mary Ann was enough to move me to tears. A grown man. I knelt down and gently gave my lovely wife a gentle kiss. When I informed her that I wanted his middle name to be Oliver because that had been her Father's name, she beamed again.

How could I not love this woman! God continued his blessings on this marriage. And I was reminded again of Rev. Birchfield's simple message of hope, "God will provide." He had heard my prayer, my plea. Let this go well for everyone. It had.

I stood up and almost blacked out. The strain I had been under was lifted and I already felt light headed and now, as I grabbed hold of the bedpost, I was reminded, I hadn't eaten anything since breakfast and night was coming on fast.

As I was leaving the bedroom, suddenly, we were invaded.. Women appeared from everywhere. They had come to visit Mary Ann and to see the new baby. Thank goodness, they brought food. Food enough to feed an army. But, I now had nourishment available.

I made my way to the dining table and, with the assistance of some of the ladies present, began to quell the hunger that had suddenly overpowered me. I scarcely knew what I was eating. I knew I was full of whatever it was.

For the next three or four days, I moved around as if in a daze. My feet scarcely touched the ground. I was assured that our new son had all his parts. He had ten fingers and ten toes. I was allowed to hold him briefly. He smiled at me. The ladies said, "That's just gas." I knew better. They could believe whatever they wanted.

Mom stayed with us, taking care of both my wife and our new son. That is, when she could get Mary Jo elbowed out of the way. Mary Jo felt as much a grandma as my own mother. Every time I was around, within minutes I was asked to leave so that something could be tended to and they didn't need me around, messing things up.

Life was like a yo yo. I was walking on air. I had a new son. I was just someone in the way. Unwanted. Rejected. It took a lot of serious praying just to get through all this.

Becoming a new father. There's nothing to it. Yeah, right. Believe whatever you want. I know better.

Since Gabriel was now safely here, I had something else to concern me. I was now responsible for the care and upbringing of another human being. I had a lot of help. I thanked God for that. A loving wife who now had another someone to love. My parents and John and Mary Jo, the "adoptive" parents of my wife and therefore they felt like grandparents, too.

Still, more than any other person, the entire future of this young man rested on my ability to be the father. One that lived up to the rules and regulations laid down in scripture for a parent and father.

People, especially the ladies, were forever saying something like, "He has his father's eyes.

He has his mother's chin.' Some part of him was always being compared to his parents.

Yes, here was a new human. The parts of two people blending together to form a new. This was, in my opinion, awesome! The miracle of God's hand at work again.

I don't like or approve violence. Neither do I like stupidity. The next person who says, "There's nothing to becoming a dad," I may smack them up the side of the head. Just a thought.

CHAPTER 16

To escape from all the females who quiet suddenly, or so it seemed to me, had invaded my domain at home and made me an outcast, I spent some extra time with the men of Twin Fork.

It was at one of these visits I was with the sheriff. It was a rainy, lazy day. Everything was quiet. Over a friendly checker game at his office which was part of the jail, my "sudden" marriage to Mary Ann came up. John chuckled. You're not the first fellow that did this, My grandfather did, too.

I had thought that, perhaps, John had some Indian blood. Now I found out that, yes, his grandmother had been full blooded.

His grandfather was a trapper. Some of these men were were called "Mountain men." I suppose that he qualified for this name.

Seems that he had spent his first winter as a trapper and had some success. He did not spend all his money on wild living until it ran out, as some were known to do. Oh, he had a few drinks and whooped it up. But then he stopped. He took the rest of his money and quietly prepared for the next winter.

He spent a lazy summer, fishing and just loafing around mostly. His stock was out to pasture. Late in the summer, they were brought in and grain fed to prepare them for the long journey and the even longer winter in the mountains. He purchased some new traps.

He knew what he had ran out of that first winter and tried to lay in extra for this winter. One horse and two mules grew to four mules and an extra horse. Salt and sugar. Coffee and flour. Tobacco and dried fruit. And, oats for the horses and mules.

Then, there was a load of trade goods. Inexpensive trinkets that were hard to obtain for the Indians he might encounter. Hand mirrors, colorful glass beads, and a number of things. He was so much better prepared for his second winter.

Going into new territory. Armed to the teeth with a rifle, a brace of pistols and knives of various sizes about his body. Still, he was one man alone in the wilderness .

Several days out, he thought that he was being watched and perhaps followed. Three days later he was sure of it. Then, just as he was beginning to really worry about it, he found himself surrounded by several young Indians.

With many signs and a few words he managed to make out, he was escorted to their village. They were friendly. Thank God. If they wanted him dead, he would now surely be gone.

He was allowed to set up his camp. Then, they took him to meet the chief. He brought gifts with him to the meeting and the chief was pleased with them and ordered that a meal be prepared for John's grandfather.

The small pouch of tobacco that had been included in the gifts for the chief was part of the mixture used in the long stemmed pipe that was lit and passed around. Between what few words of their language that he understood and the few words of English that some of them had learned, they communicated with a lot of gestures.

It was like a huge party and lasted for a couple of days. Gifts were distributed. He had a fine new pair of moccasins. A new deerskin shirt and pants. They were all happy with their prizes.

Then, as he was preparing to leave, the chief made it known that he would really like to buy one of the horses. Not really wanting to part with one of them, he instead offered one of the mules. This was not satisfactory. The Buffalo robe was withdrawn. He didn't want a mule. He wanted a horse and that was what he would have.

Seems everything had come to a standoff. Grandpa wasn't trading one of his horses for a fine buffalo robe but the chief really wanted that horse. The next offer shocked grandpa. The old chief called out a beautiful young Indian maiden, his own daughter.

Now, sons were revered by all tribes and the girls were just tolerated. This, however, was the daughter of an Indian chief. Therefore, she had greater standing and value. The chief wanted the horse. He was offering his daughter.

Now, grandpa was in a terrible spot. He didn't want to lose his good horse. But, to refuse the offer that the chief was making would be to insult the chief and could possibly cost him his life, right now. If not, the chief might just decide to run him away from the village and take everything he had. The solution was obvious.

The chief had a new horse and grand paw had him a new Indian wife. Later, grand paw said that was the best deal he ever made in his entire life.

Young Deer was to become the love of his life, his companion for all the remainder of his days on this earth and the mother of Sheriff John's own mother.

CHAPTER 17

QUIET A CONTRAST TO OUR stories. I was traveling alone, just as John's grand paw. I was going to pastor a church, without a wife and sure that some would reject a single man as pastor.

God, in his wisdom had put the two of us together. John's grand paw was traveling alone. He was facing a long winter, being all alone. I was going into a large community of people. He was leaving all signs of civilization.

Yet, our stories were so much alike. Both had, rather suddenly, became married men and both had found it to be greatly rewarding. Again, the simple words came to me. "God will Provide."

How many times I faced so many problems in my life, as a husband, as a father and as a pastor. Yet, with all my failures, and I had my share, God was always there. He never moved. I might find myself drifting away. Maybe it was just for a few minutes. Maybe it was for a long period of time. Didn't make any difference to God.

He was always right there where I had left him and willing and able to listen to my prayers.

Not only did he hear my prayers, He answered every one of them. Yes, He did that for me. Some He answered "yes." Some He answered "no." And, some He answered, "In My time, not in your time, this will come to pass."

For a long time, I had a struggle understanding this. Why couldn't God give me what I prayed for when I ask for it? Wasn't that the way it was supposed to work?

Finally, as I was reading the scriptures one day, the simple answer was right there before me.

Matthew 7: 9-11 says, "Or what man is there of you, whom if his son ask for bread will give him a stone? Or if he ask a fish will give him a serpent?

If ye then, being evil, know how to give good gifts unto your children, how much more shall your Father which is in heaven give good things to them that ask him?"

In a nutshell, it came back to that simple statement of fact to all people of faith, "God will provide." How great the message. How simple the message. How could I so easily forget the deep, abiding truth of these words?

Maybe, in God's eye, I was hungry and asking, not for fish or bread but for a stone or a serpent. God knew, even before I asked what I really needed. He wanted my asking, just as I would want my young son to ask me. It was God's delight to give to me the things necessary. Just as it would become my delight to give my son the things that were really good for him to have.

Why do we have such a struggle with some of the simple truths of the scriptures? When we feel the leading of the Holy Spirit for some task ahead, we want to answer, "Yes, but Lord - - " Do we know more than God? We know that it's impossible to say, "No, Lord." If we say "no" then he can't be Lord. He must be obeyed. However, we certainly try his patience with our answer, "Yes Lord, but - -"

God is patient. God is merciful. God, our heavenly Father, is the perfect example of what He expects his earthly sons to do as earthly fathers.

Thankfully, he is also a forgiving God. Otherwise, I'm afraid we would all stay in big trouble.

I wasn't perfect. Far from it. But I was beginning to understand the real role of an earthly father. My new biblical hero became Joseph and would remain one of my heroes until the end of my days. Chosen to be the earthly Father of Jesus. We read a lot about Mary. Consider what God wants for an earthly father.

Then, when you think of all this, think of Joseph. God said, "I want Mary for my only begotten son's earthly mother." For this we give honor and praise, as we should. Not much is said about Joseph. God said, 'I want you for his earthly father."

Wow! How great was that! With everything I felt about becoming a dad, he had to feel and so much more. Hopefully, you can begin to understand why I say he is one of my biblical heroes.

CHAPTER 18

ONE MIGHT BELIEVE THAT THIS was just a quiet town with   nothing
much going on. They would be wrong. Early in the spring, I had to
attend the funeral of a man killed down at the local saloon.

It was his own fault. No one else could be brought to blame. He
had entered the saloon with an attitude. A Mexican was working there,
cleaning the floor and minding his own business. This bully, trying to
show out for everyone present, deliberately shoved the Mexican to the
floor. "Stay on the floor or I will shoot you!" He drew his gun and found
a knife embedded in his chest and his lifeblood draining out.

Some wanted to have a hanging right there. Cooler heads prevailed.
It was self defense. There could be no doubt. I didn't try to preach the
man into heaven at his funeral. "We all preach our own funeral while
living here on earth. Nothing in his life can be changed now. We must
all prepare for the coming of the end of time for us."

Dr. Thomas Oberlin told me it was not unusual to have to patch up the bodies of those who preferred to live on the wilder side of life. This could range from stitches to broken bones.

I found that I had at least three different groups of people to minister to. One group was our faithful church members. The second group was those individuals who wanted nothing to do with God or the church.

Group three. The hard to do anything with group and seemingly the biggest group of all. They were the "Yes" group. When asked, they would quickly tell you, "Yes, I believe in God. Yes sir, preacher, you have my full support. I'll be in church next Sunday."

Yet, next Sunday never came. How do I know? Because they never made it to church. They always had an excuse. Occasionally, they had a real reason. But mostly it was an excuse.

How do you work with this group of people? They had their ready answer, "Yes sir, preacher." It never varied. There were some colorful excuses. They could be very entertaining. If they had a spiritual need, they did not hesitate. "Little Johnny is sick. Preacher, please come to our house and have prayer. We need you so bad."

Didn't matter what time it was. They were so thankful and so full of, "We'll all be at church come Sunday morning" that you wanted to shout for joy.

I soon was to learn better than to believe them. They were a part of the "Yes" group. Anything that you could think to ask, you knew the answer that was coming.

In my second summer at Twin Forks I found that I had much rather work with group two type people. They were lost. They knew they were lost. They would talk to you. They would voice their doubts and frustrations about their life. Unlike the group three, the "yes" people, sometimes I could get through to them.

With the aid of God's Holy Spirit convicting them and the group one people praying for them,

CHAPTER 19

TOBE AND I SPENT A lot of time together. Some of the church members had spent quiet a bit of time and labor on the church's buggy and it became a common sight to see the two of us out on the road as I visited church members and sought out new converts.

Tobe wasn't really happy to become a buggy horse, but I believe he consoled himself to the role. At least, he wasn't confined to the corral.

I felt it necessary to be armed when out alone, especially when I ended up far from home and darkness at hand. Most people knew about Moses' Rod and that it was always handy.

I was threatened once. Tobe and I were hurrying home when a man stepped out into the road and stopped us. I figured he had been drinking. I tried to reason with him. "Let us pass. We need to get home. Please."

Finally I reached Moses' Rod over the side of the buggy and said, "I wouldn't want you to get hurt or anything, but you are standing where I am about to shoot." When he heard me pull back the hammers, he moved and Tobe and I went home.

Sometimes Mary Ann would venture out with me on visitation. On one such visit, I met my first case of wife abuse. I knew it happened and had heard that this man might be one of those.

Mary Jo was baby sitting so it was just the two of us. As we pulled into the yard, I heard the wife say, "Watch your mouth. The preachers coming." Never could understand that. Don't people know that God hears them all the time, not just when the preacher is around?

Wasn't long after we came up on the porch and sat down that the man said, "The bible says that the man is to rule his house, don't it preacher?"

"Yes, it sure does.'

"See there woman. The bible tells everyone that the man is to be the boss. His word is law. Whatever he says, that's the way it's going to be."

"That same scripture tells us that a man is to love his wife as Christ loved the church. Now, that's a powerful lot of loving we've gotta do because Christ loved the church so much he died on the cross for it." Guess what. That didn't set too well with him.

Some people, and he was a prime example, want to pick and choose which scripture to obey and which to ignore and just hope that no one noticed or that it would simply go away. It won't.

There was sign that the wife might have been hit at some time recently. Wouldn't surprise me. She looked to be one of those shy individuals that would be easily dominated by someone who wished to do so and he surely wished to do that very thing.

Mr Brock and I were destined to meet again. He was one of those individuals who resented anyone telling him anything. In his eyes, he was a real Man's Man. He knew everything.

After prayer, we left. I'd had enough of this arrogant man to last me for a long time. How can people become so full of themselves? How can they treat their spouse, whom they have promised to love and take care of like dirt?

When we were back on the road, Mary Ann said to me, "If that fool was my husband, I'd kill him. I mean it. Shooting would be too good for him. I'd tie him up and butcher him like a hog."

I silently said to myself, "Preacher man, don't ever make this little woman angry!"

CHAPTER 20

Twin Forks cannery did a booming business in it's second year of operation. Our young student owners had survived the first year, thanks to the leadership and experience of Matthew Gibbons.

Matthew was still around and willing to help another season and we were really glad to have him. He not only had become an asset to the cannery, he worked with our church, had become an officer in our lodge and was now deep in courtship with Florence. I expected them to set the date most any time.

Around here, any female over twenty was to be considered an old maid and if they were past their twenties, all hope was lost. A male in this age group was considered a confirmed bachelor.

Trouble was, no one had told these two. If they had been married before and lost their mate, that would be one thing. But, two people well past their teen years, acting a lot like teen age kids when they were around each other. Guess real first love will do that to you, regardless of your age.

The weather was good and our vegetable crops flourished. We were all learning when to

harvest each one to assure the best flavor when it was processed. So much to learn. The shorter time between the picking and canning, the better.

We waited until the vegetables were ripe. This, too, was to assure great tasting food when the can was opened.

Almost everyone agreed with this method. Some few had to be gently reminded and this fell to the young men who were running the operation. If it was picked too green, it wasn't good. If it was over ripe, that wasn't good either. Much of this had been covered by Matthew last season, so it wasn't as big of a problem as it might have been.

Most people would resent a young man, such as we had running everything, how to harvest their crop to assure it being at it's best.

Wagon load after wagon load of freshly harvested goodies were sent south to the railroad where they were shipped to our customers over a wide area. We again had the contract for the state prison. Big, gallon size containers went to them and to any restaurant who purchased our canned fruits and vegetables.

Pint and quart sized cans went to the stores where they proudly displayed the Twin Forks label.

This brought money into the economy of Twin Forks. Not only the small farmers who were growing all that extra vegetables for the cannery, but all the people who worked there from the earliest harvest until the last one, late in the fall.

Not only did it pay everyone a reasonable amount, a sizable payment was made to help pay off the loan. The standard of living went up for everyone.

So you see, good things and bad things were happening in and around Twin Forks. Florence loaned us the cafe for our annual fish fry. Everyone, including myself ate way too much.

School would be starting soon. Then, a two week break for crop harvest and revival. Everything was moving along nicely. A bump or two in the road, but nothing to worry about.

That is, nothing until I was told that the sheriff had put one Mr. Henry Brock in jail. Mrs. Brock was with Dr. Tom. She looked terrible with cuts and bruises all over.

CHAPTER 21

Mrs Brock had made up her mind – finally. Enough is enough, even for her. She was leaving her husband and would seek a divorce. It wouldn't be easy. The law was very strict and usually favored the husband.

She had a job at the cannery and had just got her pay for the week. He had taken it from her, all of it. He thought she had more and when she didn't produce more, he had began to beat on her.

This time, he had gone too far. The injuries were plain for everyone to see and too serious to be ignored. He had followed her to the Doctor's office and this is where the sheriff stepped in and arrested him. This was Friday evening, late.

Arrangements were made for Mrs Brock to have a place to stay until Monday when the Judge would be in town. Henry managed to get word to one of his drinking buddies who considered himself to be a lawyer.

Sunday morning, with much bluster, he managed to get the old jailer to open the cell door and Henry walked out.

He had been locked up until he was completely sober and, because it was Sunday morning, the saloon was closed.

Church services were dismissed and Mary Ann and I were out front, wishing all our people good day. It was the Brown's turn to have the pastor over for Sunday dinner and we were looking forward to this.

Each Sunday, taking turns, our church family fed us. One of the perks of being a pastor and we always enjoyed the meal as well as the fellowship that this provided.

Any way, we were right in the middle of this when Henry Brock suddenly stood right in the middle of the church yard and demanded, in a very loud voice, that I produce his wife or he was going to beat the life right out of my little puny body.

Now, it's true, he was at least twenty pounds heavier than me, maybe more.

"Calm down. Lower your voice. You're standing on Holy ground. This is God's house."

With that, he let out a string of cuss words, calling me every vile thing he could think of.

"Enough is enough," I said. Before I could say anything else, Mary Ann responded in a low voice, "If you don't give him a solid whipping, I'm going to." There was no doubt in my mind that she meant every word of it.

As I stepped off the porch into the yard, he came at me with a rush, hoping to bowl me over. Didn't exactly work out that way. A short left jab right to the end of his nose said "splat" and I stepped aside. As he turned back, a solid one two combination landed above his left eye and on his nose – again. It began to bleed.

With an angry rush and shove, he managed to put me on the ground. Then he kicked me. It was a glancing blow but effective. I scrambled to my feet before he could do further damage. I faked a left and when he dodged, I slapped him right on the side of his face where the claw marks were from his wife's attempt to defend herself.

This had a terrible sting and it really made him mad. Good. I wanted him mad. I wanted him to suffer. I didn't want this fight to end. Like a good boxer, I carried him. When I thought he might go down, I'd back off. With both eyes beginning to swell and his nose bleeding, I finally decided that it was time to finish this thing.

I had not attacked his body, just his head and face. I switched tactics. A right delivered to the heart had him stopped for an instant. A solid left to the solar plexus knocked the breath out of him.

A right cross to the temple and he was out cold. I wasn't sure for a moment or two whether he was alive or not. He was. The sheriff had a couple of the men carry him back to the jail.

"If that so called lawyer shows up again, lock him up with his client and hold both of them until court." With these instructions, the sheriff left the prisoner to recover, securely locked up.

CHAPTER 22

MONDAY MORNING THE JUDGE HELD court. Henry Brock was escorted in by Sheriff John Simmons and a much subdued prisoner hardly looked up. This was the first time, ever, that he had been thoroughly beaten in a fight. His broken nose, two black eyes and the bloody gap where his front teeth had been gave evidence of the violence of our encounter.

His wife came in to testify. Then I gave an account of what had happened the day before. The Sheriff had been there and he confirmed my testimony.

Then, a surprise witness was called. The madam of our local house of ill repute took the stand. She told everyone that Henry Brock had been banned from her business due to his violent behavior.

With everything going against him, Henry offered no defense and the divorce was granted. Then the Judge ordered that he not be around his former wife or to bother her in any way.

Ninety days in state prison, suspended for three years for your behavior yesterday and all the things that happened before.

That week, Florence announced that she had agreed to become Mrs Matthew Gibbons. Plans for the wedding were soon under way.

It felt rather strange for me to be giving advice to these two. Still, I felt as if it was my sacred duty to do this for them. After all, they were facing a new life together. Different from anything that they had faced before. Many decisions had to be made and I wanted to be sure they were both on the same page.

They would have a church wedding. Nothing fancy. Just a get together with family and friends to celebrate with them as they exchanged vows. Here was one of the problems. What Matt and I and most of the men would consider simple, the lady folks didn't.

A wedding dress for Florence. Well, okay, I could go along with that. New dresses for all the ladies? Well, I suppose. And flowers, all over the church. They must have flowers. All the men's Sunday best clothes had to be clean and pressed.

A wedding reception after the exchange of vows. This would take place at the cafe. A date was set. All work was scheduled around that date. No one wanted to miss this. The entire town was practically closed. Every flower garden was missing some of their prettiest blooms.

The cannery opened back up and carried on their business as usual. Everything went smoothly there. The cafe was another matter. It was cleaned up after the reception by the ladies and then closed. It would not be open again until the couple returned from their honeymoon.

They were gone for a week. This was the time that Henry Brock made his fatal mistake. He came to the Sheriff's house and called him out, demanding to know where his wife was. As they were standing in the yard facing each other, Henry became more and more agitated.

He drew his gun and shot the Sheriff, striking him in the right shoulder which prevented him from returning fire. That's when Mary Jo stepped out and emptied her .38. Henry Brock was dead before he hit the ground.

CHAPTER 23

SEEMS THAT SHOULD HAVE BEEN the end of that. Didn't end there. That so called lawyer and drinking buddy of the late Henry Brock began hanging around Foebie Brock, widow. Apparently, he saw this as a great opportunity to stir up trouble for the Sheriff and possibly make some money.

Then, too, there was the steady paycheck from the cannery that he hoped to get his hands on and turn it into booze.

You remember Jason Fudge. A good old boy who occasionally got as drunk as a skunk and had to sleep it off in jail. Never really meant to harm any one. Just a real pest when he decided to drink the saloon dry.

His brother Jacob was an entirely different man. He liked to drink but he never got drunk. He never saw a dishonest dollar he didn't want for himself. He presented himself as a lawyer and he did have some small knowledge of the law. There was no state or federal law requiring him to pass a test or have minimum schooling. That made him a lawyer, I suppose.

Foebie missed her late husband. The further away from the date of death, the better man he became in her eyes. It helped that Jacob was around to help her remember all the good times.

They got together and demanded that a hearing be held in front of a Judge concerning the untimely death of Henry Brock and that the government pay the grieving widow for her loss.

In due time everything was set up. I was there to observe, as was several other interested citizens. Two lawyers. Overkill? Perhaps, but there was one representing the government and one for the Sheriff's department, mainly Mary Jo and John.

Jacob and Foebie sat together and she presented a rather pitiful picture all huddled up and dressed in her black.

Jacob Fudge presented his case and he was, I'll admit, very eloquent in his presentation. The late Mr. Henry Brock became a wonderful man, one who was forced to overindulge in whiskey to kill the pain caused by "that preacher" who had stirred up trouble between the loving couple.

Thank goodness Mary Ann wasn't there to hear that. I would have had to restrain her. It was bad enough that I had to sit quietly thru this.

Then he started in on the Sheriff and his allowing his wife, who had no authority, to shoot one Mr. Henry Brock.

Therefore, under the circumstances, the widow deserved a sizable payment from the government, the Sheriff's office and the church.

Suddenly, the church and I were also defendants in this case. Guess I'd have to act as my own lawyer, as I didn't have one. Court took a short recess for the other side to prepare it's case. When I mentioned I didn't have a lawyer, John's lawyer smiled and said, "I'll be glad to represent you and the church at no cost."

"Good. Thanks. When you get Mrs. Brock on the stand, be sure to ask her if her late husband ever struck or otherwise offered personal violence to her. This is the same judge that heard the divorce case and he saw the results of her being beaten."

The Sheriff was called to the stand. He was asked several questions about his job, how long he had been Sheriff and if he had been troubled by the late Mr. Brock before this incident. Yes, when he found it necessary to lock him up for beating up his wife just before their divorce.

"Now Sheriff, explain to us why your wife thought it necessary to empty her gun into Mr. Brock and take his life. On second thought, please step down and I will ask an explanation directly from your wife.

Mary Jo was sworn and took the stand. "By what authority were you outside at the time and why were you armed? Why wasn't a deputy called to help with this matter?"

"I'm usually armed when I'm expecting danger. This animal had just shot my husband and he was incapacitated due to the injury inflicted to his shoulder. I am a sworn deputy and have been ever since my husband had to transport a female prisoner to the state prison and I accompanied him. As for why I emptied my gun, it wasn't really necessary, I suppose. I got carried away. After seeing what he did to his wife, I wasn't taking any chances. Dr. Oberlin, who examined the body and pronounced him dead, will tell you that any of the shots would have been fatal."

After that, there wasn't much of a hearing left. The Judge dismissed everything. Foebie Brock and Jacob Fudge left together. There's just no accounting for what people will do or say. I had gained two more enemies.

CHAPTER 24

I HAVE FOUND THAT MY prayer life has evolved since I accepted God's call into the ministry. I began with the opening, "Lord, I want - - " whatever it was that I wanted. I want to be better. I want to deliver a stirring message. You get the idea.

The next step was to realize how selfish this must sound to God. I changed to, "Lord, I need -" and continued in this pattern for quiet some time. When I read where the scriptures said that God knows our needs before we ask, I thought "If God already knows my needs before I ask, I must be wasting a lot of time in my prayer life."

Finally, I prayed, "Lord, help me - -" and God seemed to say, "Ah, now we're getting somewhere!" No, He didn't speak to me as a person might do. But, from somewhere deep inside, I knew. Instead of trying to tell God what I wanted to do, I was now asking God what He wanted me to do.

Where do the really good, spirit filled sermons come from? From God, thru the leadership of the Holy Spirit. How does this happen? This is where it sometimes gets tricky. One must learn to listen and observe.

Here's an example. I am not enthusiastic about doing dishes. Mary Ann had been busy with a fussy baby all day. Gabriel is usually pretty good. Sleeps and eats a lot. Apparently, everything was not well in his world and he was letting mommy know about it.

I decided my sermon preparation could wait. It had been a struggle and I was getting nowhere. These dirty dishes were not going away and I should really help my dear wife. While I was doing this she said, "Thank God for dirty dishes."

"What did you say?" Shocked at such a thought, I continued to wash as she explained. "You remember our first meal together. Between the two of us there was one coffee cup, one fork and one plate. You were so generous to share, not only your food but your dishes. Now, we have plenty of food, all the pots and pans and everything else we need. I like to thank God for that every time we eat.."

"I decided many months ago to try to find something every day to simply say about, "Thank you God." This short, simple prayer has been such a revelation to me. For example, I now find it easy to say "Thank you God for the beautiful sunrise. Thank you for the beautiful sunset, the wonderful rain or sunshine or so many things and yes, Thank you God for dirty dishes.

Wow! Just like that, I had a sermon outline. "Thank you God for dirty dishes."

The Apostle Paul said he had learned to be content in whatever circumstances he found himself. I'll bet, he would have echoed my dear wife's thoughts on this. Maybe not, but I like to think that he would have.

I firmly believe that prayer doesn't have to be on one's bended knees, physically. This is a good position to place ourselves to talk to God. To be humble before him. But that's not the only way to pray.

Prayer is talking to God. Then. Being quiet and waiting on God to answer. Some of my best prayer time is in the buggy. Tobe knows the way home and sometimes he has to do most of the "Getting us home" on his own. After a visit, I may start home and start to talk to God. I can feel His Holy presence right there with me. Then, it's surprising how short a long journey can become.

After my message, I challenged my congregation to find something every day that they could really, sincerely lift their prayer to God by saying, "Thank you Lord for - - -." As for the message, I was reminded again, "God will provide."

CHAPTER 25

I CONTACTED REV. BROWNE AND discovered that he had been a very busy man since he left Twin Forks. You remember him. He was the former pastor and the one who had "Re-married" Mary Ann and me. He had established a new church in the town where his daughter lived and was their pastor.

He was delighted when I invited him to come to Twin Forks and help with revival. This would be a busy time. Harvest break at school meant two weeks to get in the fall crops, the cannery would be going full blast and we would have church every night.

Everything started with a bang. The first Sunday was homecoming and decoration which meant people would be coming from far and near as grown children who had moved away came back for a visit. The cemetery was cleaned and fresh flowers were on all the graves. Thus, decoration.

Dinner on the ground! And, the afternoon would be spent visiting and singing. Food fit for a king. No church gathering would be official unless there was adequate fried chicken, potato salad and deviled eggs. We had all that and more. Makes my mouth water every time I think about it.

For some strange reason, many people got the idea in their head that it was necessary to wait until the church had revival before any one could be born again. Where they got this idea, I have no idea. I do know that, like many other misconceptions that people have, once it becomes ingrained in their thinking, it is hard to get them to change. Well, if that's what they had been waiting on, the time was here.

Every one came to revival meeting. Sometimes, they came into the church building and sometimes they just hung around outside, wanting to be present if anything exciting happened but not wanting to be a part of it.

Also, when church dismissed for the night, there was a chance that these young lads could manage to catch the eye of some pretty lass and hopefully walk her home. Her parents would be several paces behind them and in the semi- darkness, holding hands and giggling was sure to take place.

That was some of the good stuff. For some reason, there were always a few men and older boys who thought that this was a fine time and place to bring a jug of mountain dew and pass it around. They would never dare bring the jug inside but kept it well back in the yard. Then, they would dare each other to go inside and sit.

What to do? Depended on how they acted. If they came in and quietly took a seat, nothing was said. This was usually what happened. Some dear old sister was sure to get close enough to smell their breath sooner or later.

Then, there was the loudmouth who just had to show out for everyone, right in the middle of the sermon. Thank goodness, Sheriff John Simmons was present that night. He quickly removed the rude, offensive drunk and took him to jail to sleep it off.

I had noticed that Rev. Browne had slipped away after the big dinner and visited a grave, that of his dear wife. I'm sure it was a special time for him.

The men all met before church time for a time of prayer. We could feel the Holy Spirit moving in these meetings and we were richly blessed as several new converts were born into God's kingdom. The final Sunday afternoon was a big baptizing in the swimming hole of Twin Forks.

CHAPTER 26

I asked my dad about the words on the stock of my gun, Moses' Rod. "Remember when Moses met God at the burning bush? His rod was cast upon the ground and became a serpent. When Moses obeyed God and picked it up, it again became a rod. When he was leaving that place, God instructed him to take his rod with him. Many miracles were done by God for Moses and His people involving Moses' Rod." That's in Exodus 4.

That made me appreciate my gun even more. Whether or not any miracles were preformed, my personal "Moses' Rod" might be questioned. When I think of the four stage robbers, their capture and the fact that I had somehow hit every one of them with four shots, I could see God's hand involved.

When the reward money came to the church and there was enough to finish the new church building and purchase a new piano, we were all blessed.

When Tobe and I had journeyed alone from home to Twin Forks, how much safer I had felt because of my gun. And how that man, who was blocking the road suddenly changed his mind when "Moses' Rod" made an appearance. Now, when I touch it, I feel God's presence, "I am with you."

Strange, isn't it. As Christians, we do not worship idols. We don't have wood or stone or metal objects that we hold sacred and pray to. Yet, there are so many things that we see every day that reminds us of God's presence. The sunshine and rain, the changing of the seasons. Snow. Bitter cold, where everything living and growing from the earth withers away and dies, Yet, spring comes and life again flourishes.

Some people might think it strange that a pastor, a man of peace, would carry such a gun. Shouldn't I depend on God to protect me? Moses depended on God, still, under God's instructions, he carried his rod.

We read in the 23rd Psalm, "I will fear no evil; for thou art with me." I am a firm believer that God will always look after the interests of his children. I also believe, just as firmly, that God expects us to do our part. Why should He do for us what we can do for ourselves.

As a boy growing up, I had always had a dog. That was just part of being a boy. You had a dog. Early in the spring as Tobe and I were returning from one of our visits and roaming about, I found this big dog on the side of the road, apparently abandoned. He was injured. Perhaps attached by other dogs or wild animals. Also, it was obvious that he had missed several meals.

I loaded him in the buggy and brought him home with me. I fed him and made him a bed in the barn. I discovered that he was still a very young dog. Part German Shepherd, Part Collie and who knows what else. I suspected that some of his ancestors were part wolf.

Soon, he decided that the buggy was his, that Tobe was his horse and I was simply the driver and that it was fine if I brought along Mary Ann and Gabriel. No one else. He was very jealous of his position and no one really dared to challenge him.

I named him Tony and people around town and the countryside soon knew about the preacher's new dog, the one who loved to ride in the buggy.

One afternoon late, just as we dismissed school, Dr. Tom came by. He had been out at the Killebrew ranch, the K Bar. Old man Killebrew was under the weather and wanted me to come by and see him right away.

Being a good pastor, I made haste to the barn and, after telling Mary Ann where I was going, Tony, Tobe and I made the long journey to the K Bar. As we were returning. I saw a man on the side of the road, apparently injured. When I got out of the buggy, I found I was mistaken.

CHAPTER 27

THREE RUFFIANS ATTACKED ME. I gave a good account for myself but the odds were too great. With a black eye, a sore head and multiple scratches all over my body, they had me on the ground and holding me.

'See if there is a rope in the buggy and we'll tie him up and leave him here. Bet we can get a pretty penny for this horse and buggy."

That was their big mistake. They dared to touch Tony's buggy. Apparently, he had been waiting for an excuse to join the fracas. Sixty pounds of fury exploded from the buggy. Suddenly, the odds were reversed. Taken completely by surprise, they had no answer and were soon subdued and tied up securely.

I retrieved one of the robbers pistol and fired three shots in the air. After a couple of minutes, I repeated the shots. Soon, some of the cowboys from the K Bar ranch rode up. They sent one rider back to the ranch and brought a wagon. The robbers were loaded up and away we went to Twin Forks.

Sheriff Simmons took over their care. He had to send for Dr. Tom to come to the jail and patch up several dog bites.

"Looks like they met Tony" the Sheriff chuckled as he locked them up. "They're not from around here or they would have known better."

The next Sunday Rev. Joseph Edgar Hendrix faced his congregation with a big smile and a shiny black eye and several scratches. Who said that being a preacher and pastor was an easy job with no excitement?

I was a pastor, a husband and father. I was a school teacher and an officer in the operation of our local cannery.

And, I had to pinch myself sometimes and remind myself what Rev. Birchfield had taught me: "God Will Provide."

EPILOGUE

Rev. and Mrs Hendrix lived for many years in Twin Forks, pastoring the church there and watching as the cannery made life better for all the people of the area.

Gabriel Oliver Hendrix grew up into a fine young man and in a way followed in his father's footsteps. He did not, however become a pastor. His special calling was in evangelism and going into the new century, many souls were added into God's kingdom because of his preaching of God's Holy Word.

Some parallels in our story that you may or may not have noticed. In Matthew, we read about Mary and Joseph and the birth of Jesus. Speaking of Joseph, Matt. 1:25 "And he knew her not till she brought first her firstborn."

In our story, we meet another Joseph and Mary. In a stable! Where was Jesus born? That's right, in a stable. Our couple were married in a stable, but he knew her not until later.

And, hopefully, we all learned a simple truth:

When we turn our life over to God and trust him

"God will Provide"

CPSIA information can be obtained at www.ICGtesting.com
Printed in the USA
BVOW071608060612

291954BV00002B/132/P